Worktown Words

An

https://worktownwords.uk

info@ worktownwords.uk

ISBN: 978-1-9163744-3-0

Published by Preeta Press Ltd

www.preetapress.com

Printed by ImprintDigital.com

ACKNOWLEDGEMENTS

All the pieces were initially picked by the following curators for https://worktownwords.uk

Dave Burnham: Edition 1: Theme: SPRING

Scott Devon: Edition 2: Theme: JOKER

Dave Morgan: Edition 3: Theme: HORIZON

Carol Cleary & Rita Gornall: Edition 4: Theme: ESCAPE

Lavinia Murray: Edition 5: Theme: SHOCK

Paul Blackburn: Edition 6: Theme: SILENCE

Chris Chilton: Edition 7: Theme: STRANGER

Kim Edwards-Keats: Edition 8: Theme: HERITAGE

Gareth Preston: Edition 9: Theme: CELEBRATION

Sarah Maclennan: Edition 10: Theme TEAR

FOREWORD

In April 2020, I had the idea of creating a website for new writing. Work submitted would be published fortnightly, each edition on a different theme and curated by a different guest editor. I'd like to thank them for their time and excellent work.

From the start the site seemed to be a hit with both writers and readers with all the curators commenting on the high quality and originality of the work.

After a few editions, Dave Morgan suggested that we should produce a paperback version of a selection of the poems and so, the idea for this anthology was born.

Some of the online contributors declined to offer work for inclusion here but the rest nominated at least one piece and most, we agreed, should appear here.

I hope you enjoy the variety of pieces on offer here and continue to support the website which is still soliciting and publishing new work. You can find out more about the contributors and read more of their work on the website

Paul Blackburn

Editor

https://worktownwords.uk

CONTENTS

MAGICIAN AT THE PODUIM [CELEBRATION]
Rosie Adamson-Clark

Slowly,
People emerged from behind
Closed doors,
Urged on towards
Normality,
When none was there,
The rules,
Rewritten,
Made little sense,
The new economy,
Fear,
No helium balloons,
Or kissing strangers,
The year Vera Lynn died

 Encouraged out of hiding,
The battle quietly raged on,
scientists shook their heads,
politicians continued to smile,
bending the truth,
pulling rabbits out of thin air,
they encouraged us to
celebrate,
long before the feast was ready,
those at the bottom table
left out of the planning,
gazed at empty plates
where food should be,
no streamers here,
bowls empty,
no sharing the loving cup,
punch gone.

SILENCE [SILENCE]
Linda Ashworth

Silence can mean different things to different people
A man in a busy household with many children
Can enjoy the silence of a peaceful country walk
Savouring the renewed energy that it gives him

Silence in a house with a missed loved one
Reverberates and reminds them who has gone
Filling them with loneliness and yearning
To hear the sound of their loved one's voice

Just to make them feel better and remind them
Of years gone by and people who are not there
This may be children who have flown the nest
Or that missed loved one who shared their life

In a busy job silence is not just relief but healing
Before hustle and bustle of life begins again
Let us treasure silence let it be our sustenance
Helping us as we tread life's rocky path.

ESCAPE [ESCAPE]
Phil Barling

I want to smell petrol, hear buses and cars
down Deansgate and Parkway, airport-bound for the stars
wailing and flailing into wild Friday night,
screams of delirium, screams of delight
I want to hear those Metro doors whoosh
The "How's it goin?" the "How are ya's", the whole crazy
caboose
Colliding bodies, the "Sorrys", the pub singalongs
the buskers, Big Issues, the Chuggers, the pongs
of dodgy kebab shops, of perfume and pies
Smiles wide as motorways, replacing dead eyes
I want takeaways, taxis, and train station sadness
Saturday night pre-fills, the mascara madness
reflections in shop windows open for business
the dancing, the acting, the old fairground dizziness
I want old friends and strangers, the kooky, the clowns
The crackle of barbeques in city and towns
Leave the woods to the sparrows, fed up with our chatter
Take again to the streets, to the chaos and clatter
of Bolton's big market, the barter and call
The touching, not too-muching, just closeness, that's all
I want oxygen of folk, giving life back to street
The "Hiyas", the "See ya's", the places we meet
to shake hands, hug and kiss, on a cool afternoon
I want to escape there, it can't come too soon

MY HUMAN BRAIN [CELEBRATION]
David Bateman

I sing a song of human brains
(Or would, if I could sing),
A song that says: for thinking thoughts,
The human brain's the thing!

At thinking thoughtful sorts of thoughts
Our human brains excel.
No other sorts of brain around
Could do it half so well.

And when my brain's not thinking thoughts
It's feeling feelings too:
For thoughts and feelings quite like mine,
No other brain would do.

Oh, the human brain, the human brain!
I'd have none else instead!
It fits so neatly, tucked inside
The top half of my head.

Old brains evolved in ancient beasts
Once living in the seas,
And one thing that's for certain is
That brains don't grow on trees.

Yet human brains beat those of bats
Or microbes found in cheese.
Yes, other creatures might have brains,
But not such brains as these!

Oh, the human brain, the human brain!
I've got one of my own!
My human brain, my human brain,
Inside my skull of bone!

My brain can think, it thinks a thought,
And then, when that one's done,
It only has to wait an hour
To think another one.

You don't just use it once, then flush.
There's no need to abstain,
For you can use the human brain
Again, and yet again!

Oh, the human brain, the human brain!
It thinks so hard and long.
Long may it reign! The human brain!
So soft and yet so strong!

STRANGER [STRANGER]
Bridie Breen

Always been said, a stranger is a friend not yet made.
It's the making bit that can serve us well
In all those moments, thinking alone in bed,
when emptiness threatens to cave in those walls built.
In times where reaching out, is just to be held

It tells, if there is someone to call
or anybody bothered to take the time,
to come over. Share some wine and talk
or just listen. Just listen. Just listen.
All begins with a connection

Ties forged by a smile, or eyes that meet.
Perhaps, a gathering of like-minds
sifting out commonalities. Revelling in differences.
Anything goes I suppose. Enlivened by a stance.
Questioning a purpose as words dance off the tongue.

It doesn't take long to capture the essence of a person
old or young. A conversation that reassures,
obligates a second take. Decides, there's more
to this stranger than considered before.
A portal opens up to spirit and heart
When a stranger yesterday becomes today's compatriot.

EARTHQUALKE AFTERTHOUGHT [SHOCK]
Philip Burton

Our terrier has shaken herself off.
All the shuddering now is done by us
clasping the duvet, a chair, and each other.
No collapse of roof and walls, so far,
but my all-seeing infant messenger
turns and points. "That wasn't there
that blowhole in the floorboard!"

"Just a knothole," I almost correct her
but don't; asbestos dust fountains out
in a miniature plume. Lovely in its way
till muted clicks transmute to the scream
of a misplaced cliff-ledge chick
whose breakthrough peck inside the shell
has tipped herself and egg into the sea.

We huddle in our feather bags and text
a neighbour — carpenter by persuasion —
an upright man — to advise on signs
of the imminent fall of a building. "Bless you"
he says, "witnesses are hard to find."
I hold a firm young hand and we creep
down the creased and jumbled stairs.

LONELY ROAD, LONELY PLANET [HORIZON]
Jeff Dawson

lonely road
dawn breaks, I drive aimlessly
destination far too unclear
my eyes prickle
as the sun emerges on the horizon
it's always there
but you can never reach it

in truth it's quite uncomfortable
its fingertip flames
clawing, hoping
desperate to pierce the morning mist
attempts futile, it's too cold
the atmosphere too thin
freezing my senses

is this road even open?
no cars in sight, no birds in flight
most days you can't move for people
not sure where I'm going or why I'm here
my heart is empty but my mind is clear
yet I can't see the agenda for my soul
though for some reason I exist
on this lonely road, this lonely planet

BOYS DON'T CRY [TEAR]
Andy Eycott

I feel it
the red-hot slash
as I grip my thigh
fall to the ground

knowing
that I am hamstrung

The pain throbs
pulsates, quivers
as the hammer strikes,
the nail firmly embedded.

my hands cannot hold it
cannot control or soothe it
it is a raw anguish.

You hear me, see me, help.

My heart is a muscle too
yet when I say it is torn
you say nothing
do nothing

you trivialise my torment
say I'm too young
to have feelings that strong
say my love isn't real

I say I am hamstrung,
heart strung.
You say there's no such thing.

It was just another 'thing'
that I had to unlearn,
that boys don't cry.

9

SPRING 2020 [SPRING]
Sriramgokul Chinnasamy

It's spring! Still can't be out
Haven't heard from a Wuhan friend since Lunar New Year
Another understands a panda's solitude in zoos,
whilst promising his video-calling daughter of a panda visit.
A four-year old loses her parents to the pandemic,
lives alone – neighbours feed her but can't take her home
fearing infection;
on Easter Sunday, she waits for her mum and dad.
Despite pay cuts, frontline staff support even the ones
responsible for the cuts
The definition of key workers and essentials get changed
Military budgets are secondary to health and social budgets
Other than the NHS, nothing should be "Too Big to Fail!"

NO SHOCK (draft 5) [SHOCK]
Shaun Fallows

It's a shame,
I couldn't feel shock
When the collapse of cross country Cummings never came
I wanted a bit of shock
Baying for at least 1 consequence
But what did I expect?
Again we got its none for me two for you
What they're always blooded to do
Nothing except clichéd cameo to their game

The default Is
Always our fault
Even when guiding the workers, to deaths
under brazen breaths
Backed by his band of Eton's finest clicks
They make them so dutifully like reproduced vases

All the tourists
Drab day trippers
Can have their needy nap in nostalgia
It makes no difference

 It's still a shame that most of Britain knows
The stupidly vulgar vast inequality
Its the reason I can never feel full pride in my country
Can't talk sing soundly of England's pleasant pastures

The reason I Never want to see another silly engineered scene
& Never want to meet the queen
The monarchy
The lost PPE
It's all a lie

HERO OR VILLAIN [JOKER]
Peter D Firth

When I was young it seemed that it would be easy to be a
superhero.

I just needed a bite from a radioactive spider or to inherit an
underground cave complete with man servant
and put on a mask.

The bullies who told me I was weak, would never know who I
really was.

If only family and friends knew, it would make them proud
I could fly around the moon and back to earth whenever I
liked

I could wear a rubber suit or a fancy cape and not have to
wonder if the outfit is acceptably cool this week.
I would be able to fend off the bad, turn the cruel into kind.

But what do I find?

It turns out that when boyhood dreams have faded,
I can't shoot web from my wrists or use X Ray vision (for
good!)
because my nurture wasn't a superhero recipe.

Now,
If I take off the mask you will find
The crooked smile of The Joker
Hee, Hee, Hee, Hee

LEOPARDI [ESCAPE]
James Hartnell

Giacomo sits in the family library
locked in each day till he's twenty-one
and when he emerges, a world authority
on astronomy, philology
and all the other ologies
this multilingual philosopher-poet
can't stand up straight.
He's studied too hard, his eyesight
is feeble, his back is bent,
his massive intellect crushed
by the view from the window:
his favourite hill topped by
the hedgerow that robs him
of the horizon.
And the wind blows in
from that pure infinity beyond
the gardens, the slope and the hedge
and he dreams each night of
life on the other side
and plots his escape to Rome.

JUST AS I PLEASE [SPRING]
Ian Hill

At some part of the day whenever I will
I'm quickly out the door climbing the hill
Out past the gardens verdant trimmed and neat
Wide open spaces and nature to greet
Up through the village out in open air
Sheep roam in the meadows nibbling there
Open skies and pasture mile after mile
Manicured golf course over gate and stile
Meandering trackways flow through the trees
Swaying and creaking along in the breeze
The beautiful scenery all for free
Where others walk and greet here just like me
Meandering through and over the hill
The lilies on a duck pond calm and still
Cresting on the track now and what a view
The West Pennine Moors and the windmills too
An ancient tower and a distant mill
A sense of history brooding here still
Walk by the golf course at the sixteenth green
Trespassing sheep here are eating it clean
Down into the valley out through the trees
Pause at the crossroads to go where I please
Over the railway past the ancient hall
In through the woodland out along the wall
Horses in the paddock heads nod and greet
Nibbling rabbits hopping round their feet
Down by the lakeside feeding ducks and geese
Gaggling and squawking never ever cease
Sit by the waterside where all is calm
Kids skimming stones there doing little harm
Fishermen sit there doing what they do
Others stand watching doing nothing too

Blue sailboat tacking by the farther shore
A tranquil scene I couldn't ask for more
Picnic tables outside a café door
Dogs lap water from dishes on the floor
Plodding round the lakeside back through the wood
I'd do it each day if I possibly could
Under the blue sky drifting on the breeze
Communing with nature just as I please.

HEART FELT [TEAR]
Sally James

With a flurry of kisses, he cross stitched her heart
then pulled out the thread to tear it apart.

DISTURBING THE SOUND OF SILENCE [SILENCE]
Alan Houghton

Silence is golden. Sometimes it is better when you say nothing at all. Good advice for a peaceful and harmonious life but not something to be heeded by Mam. Silent mother, that is an oxymoron if there ever was one. If something needed saying, she said it. The trouble was when something didn't need saying, she said it. The irony of it all was that while it was impossible for Mum to be silent, she could provoke a stunning silence.

Like the Sunday lunch, we were sat at the table with Mam and Dad at either end with me stuck in the middle, when Mam suddenly pipes up to my Dad "Pass the salt, you twat!". There was a stunned silence, so Mam followed up with "Hurry up, you twat!" Dad never said a word and obediently passed the salt.

Mam struggled with diplomacy at times. There was the time when she was sat next to my mother-in-law looking through my wedding album, when she suddenly came out with "You know Doris, if I had known what you were going to wear at the wedding, I wouldn't have spent as much on my outfit!" That was a real showstopper! The silence was deafening. I did an about turn and returned to the kitchen with the tray of tea and cakes that I was bringing into the lounge. There were no words that could follow that!

Or when my wife came back from the hairdressers after her first haircut since re-growing her hair following chemotherapy. "That's horrible, makes you look like a boy!" No room for sympathy or silence, just tell it how it is, Mam! Simon and Garfunkel once sang "and no-one dared, disturb the Sound of Silence". Well, Mam did. I would not have changed Mam for the world. Life would have been so much duller. Silence is not golden, it's boring. Silence is for the faint-hearted.

FREEDOM [SPRING]
Donna Hughes

The Highlands was my destination. Springtime was my
claim
A beautiful location for a princely sporting game.
I headed for remotest lochs, the salmon to engage
And left behind the ticking clocks, my office and road rage.

Deep in the lochs o'er river rocks, I cast for hours to try
To catch the fish who simply mocked my efforts with the
fly.
The darkest, deepest swirling pools reflected whorls of
light.
The shadowy dell was green and cool, then came my first
real bite.

I struck! He's on! It's him and me! That fish did fight me so.
I braced against a willow tree and let the line run low.
Then quickly I did whirl the reel in spite of drizzling rain.
I nearly had him, I could feel, then off he went again

We fought for half an hour or more my weariness was dire
The rain it eased the sun was weak but then I felt him tire.
Our fight was over very soon though winning joy was
muted

When by the stunning setting sun my rival I saluted.

Gazing at that glorious lord he saw me and he knew.
I soothed him with a gentle word then slowly I withdrew.
Heading home alone to tend to work at racing pace
I'm glad I let my glittering friend swim free in wondrous
grace.

POSTCARDS FROM AN ISLAND [ESCAPE]
Phil Isherwood

The holiday escape to be amazed again,
To dwell at a point between sea and sky.
This magnificence of nature, born out of
The Atlantic. It surely seems another world.

I stand on balconies, breathe the air that
Each cliff commands, savour intoxicating
Views from Cabo Girão or Ribeira Brava,
Vast landscapes from Miradouro da Portela.

These endless horizons convince me of
The overwhelming smallness of man. Yet
I touch the smallest flower that falls against
My hand in a crevice of this ageless rock.

We strive to explore and know this land.
Glass skywalks and lifts, places to find the
Romance. Fertile landfalls of Fajã dos Padres
Offer guava, passion fruit, avocado and fig.

Rocky beaches, levada walks, the flavours
Captured from malmsey vines, from the open
Ovens preparing espetada or scabbardfish.
Such is the richness that forms a celebration.

In the escape you forget the trials of beauty
Volcanic terrors, the storms when angry rivers
Formed their story. Memories are set free here
To leave my story in some crevice in the rock.

FROG: THE WIDE MOUTHED WONDER [SPRING]
Bernadette Jordan

I stare into the murky depths of the garden pond. There's a slow swirl of waking life. Mud stirs below. A bulging form mottled green and glistening smooth, floats then surfaces. Here he is, a bulgy eyed, bulgy bellied, bulgy thighed frog. With bulging cheeks, he croaks his rasping love song.

One morning, a cloud of burnished THE silver heaps up from the pond's surface. Frogs have spawned and I'm ever awed at plenitude. Countless cloud-like clumps, impossibly bulbous balloon with pond water. I know again the joy of spring. A fascinating mass of jelly stretches but holds together. Each ball containing a bead of life; a clumped coagulation of abundance. I watch over the days that come, see black full stops turn to commas. Jelly turns to mush and the sentence of life has begun. Tadpoles squirm, crowd together in a clump and writhe like a pit of miniature snakes. One movement sets off a chain reaction, making the water fizz with tiny ripples.

Gradually the tadpoles grow and disperse to take their chances in the far reaches of the pond. They feast on last Autumn's blackened leaves, sink to muddy depths then zip their way back up on shuddering tails to gulp air with kissing lips, leaving tiny bubbles where their open mouths break the surface.

Numbers fall, newts and dragon fly nymphs take a huge toll. But slowly, slowly a drastic change of form occurs. Legs sprout, straddling shrinking tails. Survivors crawl from the water, miniature carnivores now. A mist of midges spins a dance of life; a frog's coiled tongue springs into their midst, bringing death- to some. Each surviving frog has earned its step up the food chain.

THE SCHOLAR EATS AN APPLE [TEAR]
Helen Kay

He peeled apples as he lived.
In a study stacked with Greek myth
art, philosophy, he sheared off
a coil of yellow skin, exposing
a Crispin's naked flesh.

He cut slab-thick slices, down
to a lantern core where pips
shone like tiny flames, hardened
to amber tears whose fibrous coats
ledged in his toast-rack teeth.

Half way through *The Frogs*
juice rolled down his chin
as he seized the core, then bit
deep to crush up the seeds,
ampoules of sweet arsenic.

TIMESHOCK [SHOCK]
John F Keane

What happened here? Did someone creep inside
My mind and body? Someone fat and old?
This dimpled gut, this wheezing belly-fold,
What parts of me are these? A rising tide
Of melancholy, anger and decay?
The dried libido withers in its seed,
A wasted force; a lone, infertile weed,
An irksome imp made for another day.
The stranger settles in his new abode
And will not leave. I glimpse his sagging face
In passing windows: jowly, old and raw;
A spectre of myself that stalks abroad
And frightens children. Quickly run the days
And swifter still the waves that storm the shore.

THE DISTANT HORIZON [HORIZON]
Aldis Kreicbergs

He gazed longingly across the vast expanse of Ocean towards the distant horizon, as he had for many, many years, wondering why the Sun did not disappear in the same place that it had appeared at the beginning of the day. He sang softly to himself.

We're riding along on the crest of a wave
And the sun is in the sky.
All our eyes on the distant horizon
Look out for passers by

The song was a favourite of His Mother and Father, but he could only remember one verse. He was not sure what the words meant, apart from 'sun, sky and horizon'. He did not know many words because his parents were unable to speak to him when he was still a toddler.

He did not need words to describe what he wanted, which was to see where the sun went.

He wished he could ask his parents. They would know. His father was a wise man. He had taught him how to fish and hunt and his mother had shown him how to light a fire and the basics of cooking. He stroked his long white beard and looked across at his mother and father, who were sitting on a makeshift wooden bench, built from debris washed up on the beach. They were sitting hand in hand, looking towards the horizon. They had been there almost forever. He vividly remembered that awful day when they had sat down together, tears flowing, and fallen asleep. He had cried too, not knowing why, and laid down on their laps. He could not wake them the next morning, or for days after that. With the morbid curiosity of a child, he watched them gradually decompose, insects buzzing around, birds pecking and small crawly things burrowing. All that was left now were two bleached white skeletons draped with ragged bits of cloth fluttering in the sea breeze. Yet they appeared so majestic, sitting there, holding hands, staring out to sea. He still loved them. He had no one else to love.

He set off at dawn the next morning, knowing it would be a long journey. Provisions loaded and the ancient fishing boat patched up as much as possible but still leaking. A home-made bucket for bailing water was always stowed in the boat. He stopped paddling when the sun slowly settled into the Ocean, beyond the horizon, which seemed no closer.

He ate then slept, waking at dawn. His island home was nowhere in sight. but he knew it could not have sunk into the sea. His boat was surrounded by the vast Ocean. There was nothing but water, stretching as far as the eye could see, whichever way he turned he had a similar view, the meeting point of the sky and the sea, the horizon. He noticed that the horizon was not a horizontal line, but a slight arc, which confirmed what he had thought. He had never been to school and never learnt the words to describe what he saw, but now knew the answer. The sun and moon were round. Huge balls in the sky. He realised that he was on a gigantic globe, floating in the sky.

For the first time since his parents had drifted into their endless sleep, he cried, sobbing uncontrollably. The horizon never ended, it went on forever and ever, round and round. A great sadness welled up inside him. He had no one to share this knowledge with. He lay down and slept. It was time to join his parents.

WHO NEEDS ENEMIES? [STRANGER]
Tony Kinsella

I friended her on Facebook
At her request
A socially distant cousin I clutched to my bosom
In the spirit of the Good Samaritan
A party guest
On a quest to embarrass
And plumb unfathomable depths

I invited her
Ignited her inflammatory doggerel
Linked her into my Jacob Marley's chain of fools
Built her a platform
For her splatter-gun splutter of freeform bigotry
Caught her in my holding network
And set her free to wash her filthy laundry in a public feed
Dishing the dirt and counting headless chickens
Before they were sub-edited
A mutual friend more dickhead than Dickens
Boringly moronic
If she's got a blacklist, I want to be on it

A slithering sluice of cheap abuse
And blinkered views and bitterness
I marked her score card as she made the cut
Each cancerous mantra of bad-natured banter
'I'm not a racialist but …'

Three days ago we were perfect strangers
Now I bathe in warm nostalgia for last Tuesday
And press delete
Fantasising that it's the nuclear button

IF NOT NOW ... [SILENCE]
Dan Lever

The energetic young woman addressed Simon from his screen, her eyes wide and blazing.

"Now is not the time for your silence. Too many of you have sat in silence, for too long. When will you speak up? When will you call out these injustices? When, if not now?"

The light from the screen refracted through the tear on Simon's cheek, as Jenny passed through the lounge to the kitchen.

"Thought they'd never go down! Do you want a brew?" When Simon didn't respond, she returned, and sat on the chair arm, to see what held his attention.

"You should watch this", said Simon quietly.

"I will at some point", she replied, already moving off. "Just struggling to engage with it at the moment, you know?"

"We're all struggling", Simon whispered. "It's time to start calling this sort of thing out".

As the evening progressed, his preoccupation grew. "Going out", he snapped, grabbing his car keys. Jenny, snug on the couch, eyed him as he left, shoulders hunched.

Simon pulled over on the busy road, and examined his destination. Large house, several vehicles on the driveway. Simon hoped it was the right house. His heart was racing, and his skin felt hot, as he turned off the ignition. Abruptly, he fired the car back up again, pulling his car forward, blocking the driveway. Killing the engine, he got out, slamming his car door and striding up the driveway. He banged on the front doorframe.

He stepped back about three metres and waited. There was a ceramic teddy bear, holding an umbrella, sat alone on a shelf, high up in the vestibule, next to the interior door. Simon remained focused on that.

The man emerged from the interior door. He had reddish hair, a dressing gown, and a wary expression. He was taller than Simon, and stockier, but looked out of shape. It was definitely him.

He opened the external door, and stepped out. "Why are you banging my door down?" he asked. His tone was gruff, but calm.

"Think it's clever to swear at people in front of their kids, do you?", Simon shouted at the man, his voice squeaking slightly on 'do you'.

The man's bafflement was plain. "Fuck are you on about?"

"All I did was block your driveway, and you come out effing and jeffing at me in front of my kids! See that car, blocking your driveway? Why don't you ask me to move it now, eh?" Simon's voice sounded tight and high to his own ears, like he had inhaled helium. The man smirked at him. "Ok, can you move your car please?", he asked, all mock politeness.

"Get fucked, you prick!"

The man looked Simon square in the face for a long beat, then rolled his eyes, exhaling loudly. "Listen pal, I've no memory of this, but I get a lot of people blocking my driveway. When even was this?"

Simon swallowed hard, and answered, "It would have been about six weeks ago, round the beginning of May".

"May?!" The smirk was back. "What did I say to you, back in May?"

"I can't remember the exact words you said!" barked Simon. The man looked at Simon and began to bray with laughter. He bent over slightly, placing one hand on his knee. A curious thing was starting to happen to Simon. His pumping heartbeat slowed. He felt himself begin to disassociate with what was taking place. A strange serenity blossomed within him, the dispassionate bystander observing the scene.

With a long theatrical sigh, the man straightened. He shook his head slightly at Simon and said, "Get off my drive, you tosser".

Simon had planned his moves on the way here. Stepping forward, he thrust his elbow into the man's nose. The man sat down abruptly, clutching his face in both hands. Blood dribbled from between his fingers, falling in fat round spatters on the block paving between his knees.

A muffled sob alerted Simon to the little girl. She was stood in the vestibule, ginger pigtails and Peppa Pig pyjamas. The heat abruptly drained from Simon's skin, as both men listened to the little girl quietly crying.

Simon sat in the holding cell. The police had found him sat in his car at the scene, waiting. He had moved the car backwards, out of the way of the driveway.

An officer entered. "Mr Williams has dropped the charges. You're free to go. Your wife is waiting at reception for you".

Jenny's mouth was so tightly compressed her lips had disappeared. "What the fuck, Simon", she muttered furiously, on the drive home. They pulled up at the lights, next to a dark shiny BMW, hip hop blasting. Simon kept his eyes on the windshield in front of him.

IN A QUINK OF TIME [HERITAGE]
P.A. Livsey

After her fracas on the ferry we walked on tenterhooks.
Shuffled amongst locals – over newly laid tracks.

Some of us steeped deep into the book of Kells.
Perched in O'Neil's, drank Guinness, ate victuals,

gazing at Molly and musing; that ink never dries
in a poet's home where a ballad holds its breath.

Crossing the flat-back of O'Connell's, we marvelled
at a Galleon glazing on the compass of movement.

Strode on to where freedom's fragile web was fought
for at the GPO, as the city ached in its belfry.

Back at the port, we left with our history clinging
to our bones and friendship's threads unravelling.

CATHEDRAL POET IN EXILE [SILENCE]
Julia McGuinness

Abbey Square cobbles are fists
under my shoes. I don't miss them,
nor those mornings of organ-tuning,
the air slabbed with rising notes
of random length. Abrupt stops.
St. Werbergh's Shrine sighing.

And I hadn't thought about
candles lit in Chapel harbours,
bright glass gaze of angels, saints,
Choir's wooded stalactite parade,
till I stood where branches arch
over this bluebell-peppered glade.

Trees touch fingertips in prayer.
Sunlight's dapple dissolves words.
Air drifts in an incense of silence.
I am held in canopied sanctuary,
taste again that poise of space
that shimmers at the brink.

TEARS OF A CLOWN [TEAR]
Phil McNulty

I'll always be the lad
In the coffee bar,
The Wimpy, El Cabala,
The Covered Wagon.
The tremor and palpitation
Of night time.
Bright lights,
The scooters and girls on pillions.
There's no me
No you
When you're In a gang,
Terrified to dress out of place,
Put the wrong song on the juke box,
Which isn't
Smokey or Freda Payne,
And for tobacco fog to fill the chasm
Between us and the girls.
Some were bad girls,
With bad names we made up
To label our fear.
Others were
Delicious,
Like the burgers
We never had the money to buy.

THE SLOW TUMBLE OF CLOUDS SIDEWAYS
[SILENCE]
Michael Murray

The slow tumble of the clouds sideways
across the blue sky's bald pate,
lit and then obscured. It had been dark
in me all day, and then I realised:
I had no windows wide open in me
like these.

The nine-thirty flexi-time work cut-off,
while high above the miles of cloud
gathered, moved huge weathers.
The scale was constantly changing;
the scurrying of our smallness,
the huge slow masses.

Sometimes it seems our lives are lived in words
all scurrying together; vocabularies
like clouds, huge, full
of everything that sustains us.
So why these snarl-ups on the road:
why this darkness in us;
these stops?

I have sent words out, scurrying little helpers,
to draw you back from harm, with a busy
tie-ing in of reasons for continuing.
And I have stood there too where words fail
at the roof edge, face to face
with that wordless place
as big as the sky, and as hungry.
It has nothing to say that words can understand.
And everything to mean.

INTRUSION [ESCAPE]
Jenny Palmer

I stray from the path
tread through ramson and bluebells
down the slope to the brook
Rotting tree trunks provide comfort
as I sit among saplings
newly planted to shore up the bank
and slow down the flow

On summer days
our favourite pastime
to escape the heat
and our mother's clutches
was to go paddling in the brook
to wade up to our knees
in ice-cold water

I am tempted
to cast off my shoes and socks
let the water trickle between my toes
I hear branches crack overhead
Two sika deer leap out, startled
disappear over the ridge
an emptiness lingers

STRANGER [STRANGER]
Marilyn Payne

Andrea sent me a friend request on Facebook. I didn't know her. She was a stranger to me, but, if she's a friend of Barbara's, whom I have known since childhood, I trusted she would be a decent person. We communicated through Facebook initially but then we spoke to each other on WhatsApp, on a one to one basis. She became less of a stranger to me and more of an acquaintance. She lived in the same town as myself, so we could relate to each other on local issues. Then Covid 19 hit and we shared concerns for our friends and family. We both had health issues so could empathise with each other.

My daughter contracted the coronavirus and I was very worried about her and Andrea was concerned for my daughter and also me, as a mother. She texted me almost daily. During Lockdown Andrea and I had to order groceries online. Andrea went to bed about 10 p.m. each evening, always tired with her health issues. However, this was the best time to find a delivery slot on Asda's website. I tended to look on the website each week for both of us and inform Andrea of the available slots.

"What would I do without you?" She laughed.

"Starve!" I replied, jokingly.

One day we agreed a time when we would chat on the telephone and we talked for hours. On several occasions we spoke for long periods. During this time, I found out Andrea is a keen animal lover and doesn't hold back with her opinions on animal cruelty. It makes sense she is also a vegan. What doesn't make sense to me though, is how she loves snakes. I just don't like the look of them. I don't find them attractive creatures at all.

During one of our texts, Andrea laughed. "I will introduce you to Tommy one day".

"We'll see." I replied, not convinced.

During lockdown Andrea agreed that staying home wasn't a big deal for us. Our health issues had kept us at home anyway. However, we both acknowledged our routines had gone to the wall and we were becoming quite lazy. We promised each other we would get stuck in to projects. Hers was the garden and mine was writing.

Over the next five days I wrote something, anything, on a daily basis. I attended a writing group on Zoom, where I got inspiration from the tutor and members of the group. I actually got stuck into housework!

I realized I hadn't heard from Andrea for five days. I assumed she was busy also. I sent her a text via WhatsApp and I wasn't prepared for the reply.

"My brother's died. It was unexpected. I am in shock. Devastated."

I felt physically sick. Whilst I was trying to process the information, Andrea texted again.

"Can I ring you tonight?" She asked.

"Of course you can. Andrea, I am so sorry".

"Thank you. Is eight o' clock ok to ring?"

"Yes. So sorry Andrea. Speak later"

We spoke for hours. Well into the early hours. She spoke of her shock at hearing of her brother's death, the unexpectedness of it all and the frustration, hurt and anger she felt for losing him.

We spoke many times after that, for long periods. Andrea supported me when my daughter had the coronavirus and I am supporting her with her grief and the difficulty of being partly responsible for organizing a funeral, with her health issues and in the current Covid 19 climate.

We haven't yet met but we both agree that we are good friends now and our friendship will grow stronger. So, a stranger became an acquaintance and is now a firm friend, thanks to our mutual friend Barbara and the power of social media.

DARKNESS: MY OLD FRIEND [SILENCE]
Jacqueline Pemberton

Absence of sound,
Unrealised bliss,
Echoless emptiness
Where everything
And nothing is possible.

A distant tap on cave walls
Will set my heart in motion.
Must I dance to its beat?
Allow blood to pulse through
A virgin forest of arteries
And willowed bone?

 If I held the power
To stop it all and never
Open my ears to the cacophony
Of the living or expose
My eyes to the sear of daylight,
Would I consent to birth?

Or would I remain
In the un-breathed darkness
Of unformed flesh,
My voice forever muted,
My story never known?

SPRING CLEANING [SPRING]
Gillian Popplewell

I've washed all the curtains
Washed all the blinds
Washed all the paint-work
That the side-board hides.
Washed all the lamp-shades
Washed all the bed sheets
Washed the shower curtain
Where soap and scum seeps.
All of that washing, all of that soap
Washing in readiness
For Spring's renewed sense of hope.

I've steam-cleaned the carpet
I've shaken the rugs
Laundered the duvet
Disturbed all the bugs.
Removed all those bin bags
Disinfected the drawers
Rotated that floor mop
On the lino – on all fours.
All of that shaking, all of that elbow grease
Shaking in readiness
For Spring's spiritual release.

I've dusted the T.V.
I've dusted the table
Dusted nooks and crannies'
As far as I'm able
I've dusted the staircase
I've dusted bed-heads
I've dusted the corners

Where daylight seldom treads.
All of that dusting, all that bees-wax
Dusting in readiness
For Spring's renewed tracks.

I've cleared out my wardrobe
Jumpers semi-retired
I've cleared out my undies
Thermals not required.
I've cleared out the freezer
Salad days lie ahead
I've bleached that old tea-pot
Filled the ice-tray instead.
All of that clearing, making room for the new
As my mind, soul and body
Await Spring's glorious view.

LAUGH, CLOWN, LAUGH! [JOKER]
Kathleen Proctor

With a rictus smile upon my face,
I cavort, juggle, tumble to order.
The audience disposed to mindless laughter.
I hate all of them. The happy families
With their contented lives, their fat children
Stuffed with burgers and hot dogs.
Look at me. Stupid face, stupid clothes, stupid life!
Another custard pie, another silent scream.
Another pratfall and I just want to stay here,
Prone, sinking deeper into the sawdust.
A seething mass of disgust revulsion and regret.
I clip clop on with my outsize shoes,
Grasping my bundle of red balloons.
Each will explode, like a gunshot in my head,
Leaving behind only useless, collapsed detritus,
Like the pathetic remnants of my life.
I grin, but I cannot bear it.

SOMETHING TRANSMITTED [HERITAGE]
Alanna Rice

Searching for markers, identity
to fulfil a need to be positioned amidst the monochromatic
maelstrom of affirming whose lives matter:
can I be found in the twisty dark mixed curls of my noble son
or hidden in the surround of my fair Grannie's sun-killed
arms?
Am I carrying it in the strong, shapely legs of my paternal
sweet-souled grandmother, or perhaps it
stems from my tall mocha grand namesake who proudly
speaks of Arawak genes.

These big sepia eyes (from the mother who sees everything
and gifted ocular symmetry to her daughters and another
curly-headed grandson) look back at me blankly as I
Question

whether it can be found in the culinary always-too-many-
dishes spreads I have prepared, hidden in the spices, smells
and secret auntie recipes.
Am I finding it in the newly natural textures of my resembles-
me hair during Wash Day?
I search the reflection of the carbon copy image of my father
during our Atlantic-crossing video call, hopeful for a clue.

I change direction and ponder whether it is less internally,
genetically determined and could it be shaped by the
mountainous gap year, the riotous years running amok in the
cobbled streets of a roman city. Was there a bend in this
malleable legacy from the BL postcodes during the recent
crystal years?

Finally, my thoughts land on the cultural inheritance I share with my pre-schooler son in this new island life I yearned for and manifested? I listen for the answer as he walks down the stairs singing take me to the river in pure Talking Heads tones.

WHERE THE HEART IS [HERITAGE]
David Subacchi

To awake to the sound of wind whistling
Between the chimneys of a coastal town
And the scream of seagulls as rain beats down
On slate rooftops and cast iron guttering
To rise and to hear milk bottles tinkling
On doorsteps where delivery men frown
Awaiting payment for bread white and brown
Drawing on cigarettes and muttering.

To thrill to the call when Sunday bells ring
In an old, stone-built church that stands nearby
And join with the worshippers as they sing
Praise and thanksgiving to our God on high
To be home again where memories cling
Home where the heart is under a Welsh sky.

MARTIN MERE WETLAND LANCASHIRE.
[HERITAGE]
David Selzer

Before the marsh on the coastal plain was drained -
to turn the dark, rich glacial soil
into the broad fields of market gardens,
selling fresh produce south to the port city
burgeoning daily from mouth to mouth -
the mere was vast, eight square miles and more.

Family groups wandered the margins -
to fish, collect eggs, snare birds. Settlements
became hamlets, became villages:
cutting the reeds for thatching, cutting the peat
for cooking fires from the ice age bogland.

The long orangey-pink streaks of sun setting
over the Irish Sea turn the lake
from silver to pewter, and the birds
to cut-outs. A two carriage commuter train
crosses at the furthest edge, its windows
rectangles of bright yellow in the twilight -
as the watchers in the hides observe,
in a barely whispered wonderment,
thousands of pink footed geese appear.

They are wintering here from the breeding grounds
in the mountains of Iceland and Greenland -
by day feeding on stubble fields, in the dusk
settling noisily on these dark waters
with their poignant, slightly throaty calls,
their myriad wings black in the fading light.

BEYOND THE HORIZON [HORIZON]
Craig Snelgrove

You only know you've gone past it
once you've gone past it.
As it turns out, there isn't much.
You're more or less in the same place.
It's the exact same town, in fact,
full of replica streets,
downbeat, disheartening streets,
streets you've walked your whole life.

You've done everything you never wanted to,
been everything you ridiculed
before your descent over the horizon.
You signed on for a year or so.
You let a job keep you
after becoming scared of the alternatives.
You worry about your health a lot.
 You often think to yourself,
"If only I could go back,
go back over the horizon,
free to just be myself again",
                                  but then,

early one evening,
someone comes to you
with a cigarette and a milky brew,
and they kiss you on the forehead, gently,
and you know the old days are gone,
you'll never go back over the horizon.
It could be worse,
                        couldn't it.
You know it.
                  You know it for a fact.

THE SPRINGER [SPRING]
Hilary Walker

We waited until spring
in need of a special day to say goodbye
a day we felt she would have chosen

Clear blue sky, leaves unfolding in surprising warmth
and the familiar scent of beginnings
the return of life
blended with nature's secrets

She was a runner,
from an early age she craved freedom
a walk around the block wouldn't do
it was running or nothing

She flew fast, over the fields beyond the hedgerows
through the woods at top speed somehow just missing
the tips of shoots and saplings
excitedly bounding forward, heading up high onto the
banking
a pause for a moment in the cool stream
and a look on her face that said
'this is why I'm alive'

She was more than a dog and she knew it
she had no time for mere mortals or animals
she was her own woman,
a canine princess who left us before winter solstice arrived
dark days to survive

We waited until spring to say farewell
releasing her tearfully into a flawless sky

recalled clearly in our mind's eye her perfect presence in our
lives
the gift that she was
the lessons she taught
running free and the glory of being alive

THE INEVITABLE STRANGER [STRANGER]
Jack Dorling

On a deserted beach, gazing across the endless ocean
The view was intoxicating, he was choking with emotion
His face was weathered with the ravages of time
Growing old gracefully had been his only crime
His eyes were fixed solely in an out of range stare
He stands in silence knowing he has done his share

Way out over the ocean, he makes out a ghostly shape
It is slowly moving closer, gesturing for him to escape
He knows there is one final journey that has to be tackled
alone
Has his time come to encounter the great unknown
The stranger inches nearer, offering a brotherly hand
The old man ventures forward as his feet lift of the sand
The stranger looks familiar, as he sinks into his embrace
Is it some ancient relation preparing him to displace
He closes his eyes slowly, conditioned to face the end
Knowing the inevitable stranger is now his inevitable friend ...

RETRIBUTION [SHOCK]
Dorothy Snelson

Shock. Horror!

Did Jimmy really say that? Did we hear right? Did he truly say that terrible word that must never be spoken? Did he definitely say 'bloody'?

Miss has him by the ear and he is out to the front of the class. She addresses us sternly saying

'We shall soon see what happens to boys who swear' and with that she leads Jimmy from the room.

We sit in silence dreading what is to come. A class of four and five year olds in 1940's Westhoughton.

Soon they are back. Jimmy is carrying a clanking metal bucket. Miss has a gym mat, a scrubbing brush and a block of carbolic soap.

Our eyes widen in shock as we try to anticipate what is to come.

Like the sacrificial lamb Jimmy is made to kneel on the mat. Miss flourishes the scrubbing brush and dips it in the water and applies the soap.

'Anyone who swears' she says melodramatically 'has their mouth scrubbed with carbolic soap. That teaches them never to swear again.'

Jimmy is crying loudly by now and he is not the only one. We are all upset and frightened.

Miss lingers a terrifying few minutes for effect before putting down the brush and telling Jimmy to stand up.

'This time you are very lucky Jimmy. I am going to let you off. I won't be so lenient next time. Take the bucket back to the kitchen.'

The class heave a collective sigh of relief. I have wet my knickers and I'm not alone.

Was it the right way to teach us a lesson? You decide.

FADING BY [SILENCE]
Lynn Walton

she shuffles on toasted sand
carries her world with knotted hands
watches the rhythm of tides
with struggling eyes
wanders this beach
with stuttering feet
 the sea scuttles in
snatches her footprints
rinses her away
with waves of applause
and splashing encores
smudging her outline
drowning her timeline
muffling her soundtrack
pushing her words back
they dissolve unsaid
on lips unread
 but the girl inside her still smiles
through the tangle of lines
binding her face
as she remembers the man
who gathered her in his gaze
loved her in this place
combed promises
through her salty hair
 she listens for the voice of him
forgets why she cannot find him
 his blush still flushes her cheek
a lantern in her downpour

HEARTS [JOKER]
Rebecca Shivji

With shuffled deck of cards
clutched within clean hand,
it occurs, how Government
lockdown is
fulfilling objective of
distancing people physically.

But, a need for patience
as time fans.
And choosing a card
to occupy my mind,
the joker appears.
Game dependant
this could be
good or bad.

In similar vein,
some people are viewing
this imposed quarantine as a trump,
due to seeing themselves as
safe at home;
while others are struggling
with the mental distress, of being stuck at home.

Either way, Old Maid,
cautions how
jokers ought to be
avoided - this isn't a game that
anyone wants to lose.

Remembering the joker's wild.
I change the card
to hearts.
A symbolic suit with the power to
connect us -
to all those we love,
those on our street, in our town, our country, and
worldwide.

Together,
our hearts hold a shared hope.
That Covid-19,
the invisible killer,
will soon falter
and fail to spread further;
especially when so many of us
are showing that we care,
by adhering to the rules, and
temporarily staying
apart.

SONG OF MYSELF [HERITAGE]
Lavinia Murray
Or, the adventures of the frozen embryo

I'm in the double-walled waiting room for a womb
on a micro-polar generic afternoon
the air folds its ghostly fingers with the cold
it grasps at nothing, aka me, there's nothing much to hold
I'm very young but my young is very, very old

kipping in the company of both ancient and modern winters
spelling ETERNITY with a slew of icy splinters
hoping to arrive after some annunciation
following a decade of brusque uterine rejection
they'll call me implant but that's a misconception
rather ubermadchen-ubermenschen
ker-pow-ering through a neat c section

ah, *if* I'm born, whose parting breath will I breathe first
whose milk of human kindness start my thirst
I'm very upbeat although staring at the void
a court injunction dictates I'm soon to be destroyed
don't much fancy being bio waste
don't want hot tongued deletion to have a little taste

toggle me in the google other-earthly map
easter-egg me on a metaphysical pre-soul app
don't know what's circling in my chromosome whirlpool
monsters of kindness or angels that are cruel

I'll escape disguised as chewed bubble-gum or cheese
make cash from unborn people-trafficking in bags of frozen
peas
twirl my umbilicus like a boomboom-bah bull-roarer

49

wear my placenta full tilt like a cocked fedora
hook up with liberated cryonic human heads
propped by their neck stumps on their pedestal deathbeds
they'll grant me external hard drive memory
to make a fuller, longer, chorused song of me

in fact
I'd free all ice capped bonces and go tete a tete
and make myself a fast sloe, never frozen internet

oh heritage, I am my own
a human thing as yet unsown